Dedicated to my son, Christian.
You are everything you say you are. Speak life!

ISBN: 978-1-955574-15-0

For more books, visit us online at www.sableinspiredbooks.com

I Speak Life

A Book of Affirmations for Boys

By Shayla McGhee

I am
generous.

I am
healthy.

I am helpful.

I am
imPortant.

I am inquisitive.

I am inventive.

I am
Joyful.

I am loved.

I am
proud.

I am responsible.

I am
smart.

I am successful.

I am
super.

I am
talented.

I am
thankful.

I am
unique.

I am
patient.

About the Author

Shayla McGhee

Shayla McGhee is the owner and operator of Sable Inspired Books and Ivory Pen Publishing. When she is not writing, she enjoys traveling and spending time with her family and friends. Find out more about Shayla's upcoming works by following her on Instagram @mcgheepartyof5 or visiting sableinspiredbooks.com.

www.sableinspiredbooks.com   Facebook: @sableinspiredbooks   Instagram: @sableinspiredbooks